LEVEL 2 SCIENCE
LET'S READ AND FIND OUT

HOW DEEP IS THE OCEAN?

BY KATHLEEN WEIDNER ZOEHFELD

ILLUSTRATED BY ERIC PUYBARET

HARPER

An Imprint of HarperCollinsPublishers

Special thanks to Dr. David Gruber, a marine biologist at the City University of New York
and the American Museum of Natural History, for his valuable assistance.

The Let's-Read-and-Find-Out Science book series was originated by Dr. Franklyn M. Branley, Astronomer
Emeritus and former Chairman of the American Museum of Natural History–Hayden Planetarium, and was formerly
co-edited by him and Dr. Roma Gans, Professor Emeritus of Childhood Education, Teachers College, Columbia University.
Text and illustrations for each of the books in the series are checked for accuracy by an expert in the relevant field.
For more information about Let's-Read-and-Find-Out Science books, write to HarperCollins Children's Books,
195 Broadway, New York, NY 10007, or visit our website at www.letsreadandfindout.com.

Let's Read-and-Find-Out Science® is a trademark of HarperCollins Publishers.

Library of Congress Cataloging-in-Publication Data
Zoehfeld, Kathleen Weidner, author.
  How deep is the ocean? / by Kathleen Weidner Zoehfeld ; illustrated by Eric Puybaret. — First edition.
  pages cm — (Let's-read-and-find-out, Level 2)
  ISBN 978-0-06-232820-5 (hardcover) — ISBN 978-0-06-232819-9 (pbk.)
  1. Oceanography—Juvenile literature. 2. Ocean—Juvenile literature. 3. Children's questions and answers.
I. Puybaret, Eric, illustrator. II. Title.
GC21.5.Z64 2016   2015018471
551.46—dc23   CIP
                                                                                                         AC

The artist used acrylic on paper to create the illustrations for this book.
Typography by Erica De Chavez
16 17 18 19 20 SCP 10 9 8 7 6 5 4 3 2 1
❖
First Edition

For Brian—K.Z.

For Antoine and Claude—E.P.

At the beach, it's fun to splash and play in the ocean waves. Seashells sparkle in the sunlight. Seaweed gets tangled in your toes.

You can watch your feet wiggling in the water as you wade out. Ankle-deep! Knee-deep! Waist-deep!

Look into the distance, and there's ocean as far as you can see.

9

Ocean covers almost three-quarters of the Earth. Near the shore, the water can be shallow enough for wading. But as you go farther out, it gets deeper and deeper.

If you want to explore the deep water, you're going to need some **scuba** gear!

You put on a waterproof mask so you can see underwater. You strap an air tank on your back for breathing and fins on your feet to help you swim faster. You dive down. The water is blue and lit by the sun above. You see fish and crabs, snails and clams, and so much more!

Hoses bring air from your air tank to your mouthpiece.

11

All this colorful life depends on the plants of the sea—the seaweed that grows near shore and the tiny **phytoplankton** that float and swim in the open water.

Most phytoplankton are too small to see without a magnifying glass or microscope.

Diatoms

Cyanobacteria

Kelp greenling

Dinoflagellates

Coccolithophores

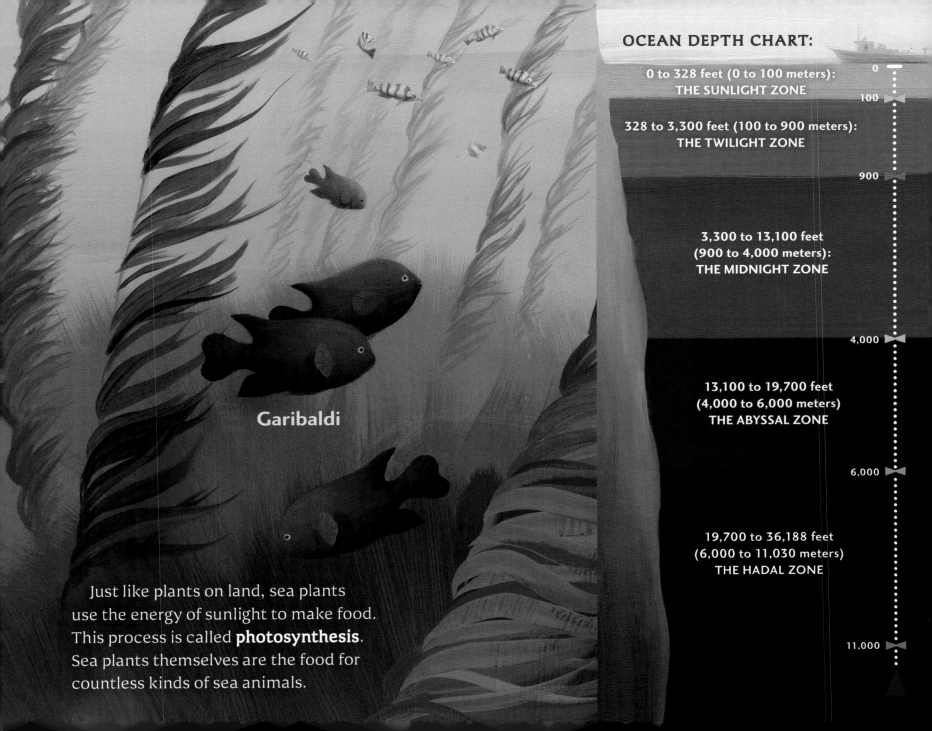

Garibaldi

Just like plants on land, sea plants use the energy of sunlight to make food. This process is called **photosynthesis**. Sea plants themselves are the food for countless kinds of sea animals.

OCEAN DEPTH CHART:

0 to 328 feet (0 to 100 meters):
THE SUNLIGHT ZONE

328 to 3,300 feet (100 to 900 meters):
THE TWILIGHT ZONE

3,300 to 13,100 feet
(900 to 4,000 meters):
THE MIDNIGHT ZONE

13,100 to 19,700 feet
(4,000 to 6,000 meters)
THE ABYSSAL ZONE

19,700 to 36,188 feet
(6,000 to 11,030 meters)
THE HADAL ZONE

0
100
900
4,000
6,000
11,000

You kick your fins and swim deeper. About one hundred feet (30 meters) down, you may notice it's getting darker. The sun looks like a lamp far overhead.

At the beach, the water felt warm on your toes. Here, the water feels much colder. This far down, the pressure of the water on your body is getting uncomfortable, too. Water is much heavier than air. You can feel the water squeezing you. You feel it most in your ears and chest. Scuba divers rarely dive deeper than 130 feet (40 meters). That's about as deep as a twelve-story building is tall. Beyond that, the pressure becomes almost too great for humans.

Expert science divers use special equipment to swim down as far as 500 feet (150 meters). At that depth, you will see hardly any plants. Phytoplankton struggle to live in this dim environment. With only a little sunlight, photosynthesis becomes almost impossible. With few plants to feed on, there are fewer fish and other animals.

If you want to see what lives deeper than 500 feet, you'll have to climb aboard a **submersible**. It has strong metal sides to withstand high pressure. It's heated to keep you warm. And it carries air, so you can breathe.

Safe in your submersible, you dive down, down, down. Outside your window, you see only inky darkness. Hardly any sunlight can reach this far through the water.

Moon jellyfish

Ocean sunfish

Pink helmet jellyfish

Orange roughy

Larval eel

YOU HAVE REACHED THE TWILIGHT ZONE.

You turn on your searchlight and scan for any sign of life. You spot a few jellyfish. Below 660 feet (200 meters), many animals have jelly-like bodies. Jelly animals are nearly invisible in the dim light here. This helps them hide from enemies or sneak up on prey.

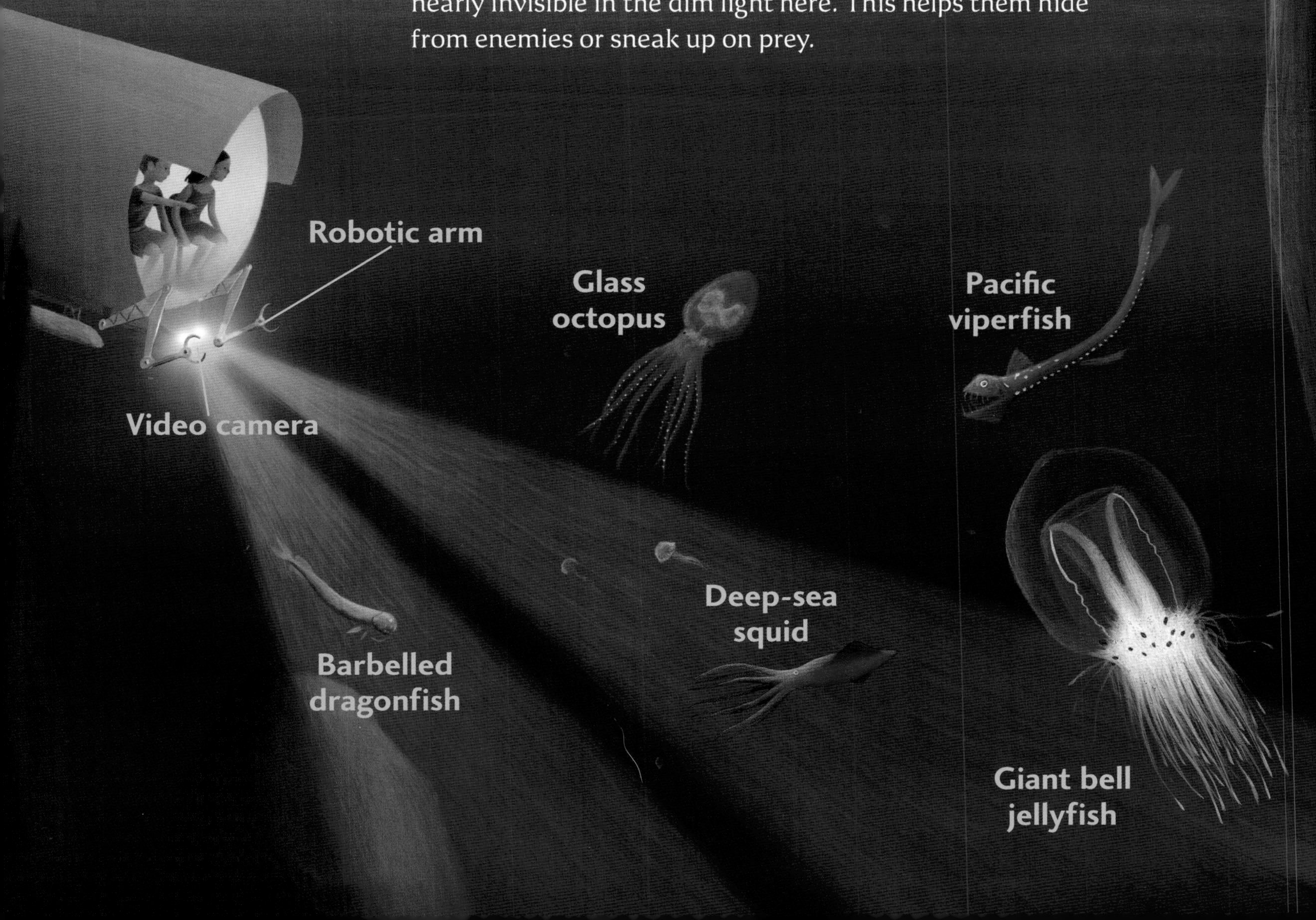

Robotic arm

Glass octopus

Pacific viperfish

Video camera

Barbelled dragonfish

Deep-sea squid

Giant bell jellyfish

17

Some of the biggest animals in the world live down here too. Giant squid prowl the deep. They use their long tentacles to grab fish. A squid as long as a school bus looks pretty scary. But something even bigger hunts for them. The sperm whale—the largest predator in the world!

The giant squid has the largest eyes of any animal on the planet. Those big eyes may help the squid spot its enemy in the dim light.

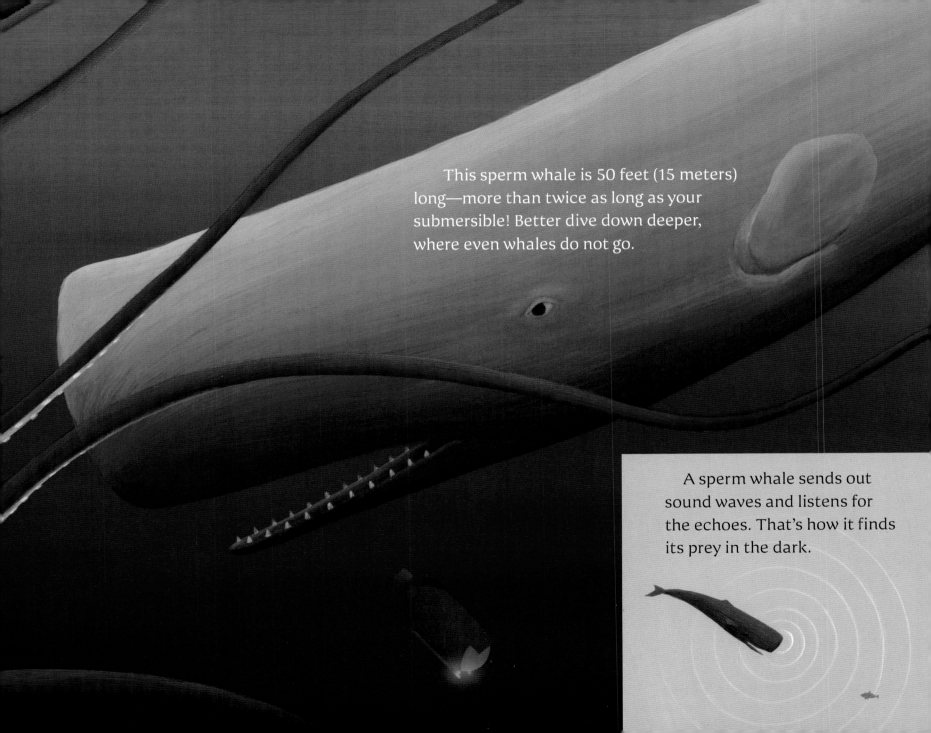

This sperm whale is 50 feet (15 meters) long—more than twice as long as your submersible! Better dive down deeper, where even whales do not go.

A sperm whale sends out sound waves and listens for the echoes. That's how it finds its prey in the dark.

ENTERING THE MIDNIGHT ZONE

Around 3,300 feet (1,000 meters)—just over half a mile down—there is no light at all. Before the first submersible was invented, scientists weren't sure if anything could live for long in such darkness. But now we know many types of creatures are at home here.

Although there's no sunlight, there is animal light—or **bioluminescence**. On land, fireflies and glowworms make their own light. Here, thousands of different types of fish, jellies, shrimps, octopuses, and other animals do.

Vampire squid

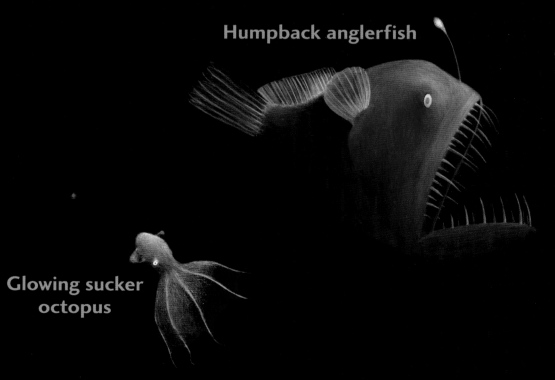

Humpback anglerfish

Glowing sucker octopus

Strawberry squid

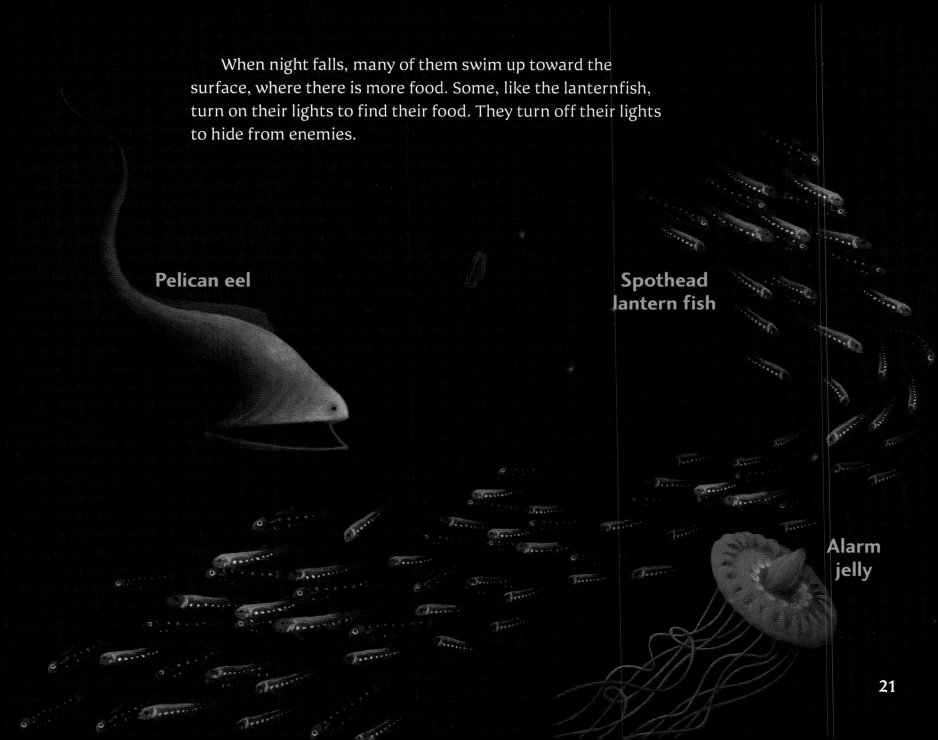

When night falls, many of them swim up toward the surface, where there is more food. Some, like the lanternfish, turn on their lights to find their food. They turn off their lights to hide from enemies.

Pelican eel

Spothead lantern fish

Alarm jelly

You take your submersible down even farther. At around two and a half miles (4,000 meters) deep, you see a muddy plain below you. You have reached the bottom. Scientists call it the Abyss.

The deep ocean floor makes up more than half of the Earth's surface. But we know very little about this area. More people have traveled into outer space than have been down this far.

Sea urchin

Glowing sea cucumber

THE ABYSSAL ZONE

At first it looks like there are no animals here. But look closely and you see tracks and trails everywhere. Brittle stars, sea urchins, and sea cucumbers crawl over the mud. They eat tiny particles of dead plants and animals that have drifted down from above.

You glide over the seafloor, scanning with your searchlight. There are many tracks but only a few animals. Each animal wanders far to find enough food in the mud.

Tripod fish

Brittle star

23

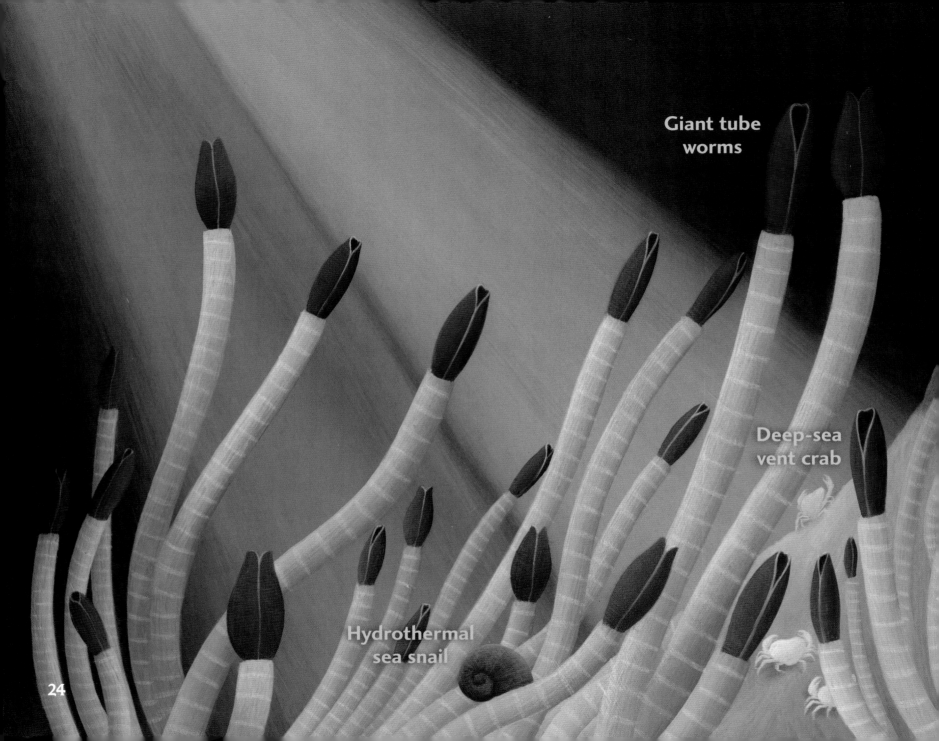

Giant tube worms

Deep-sea vent crab

Hydrothermal sea snail

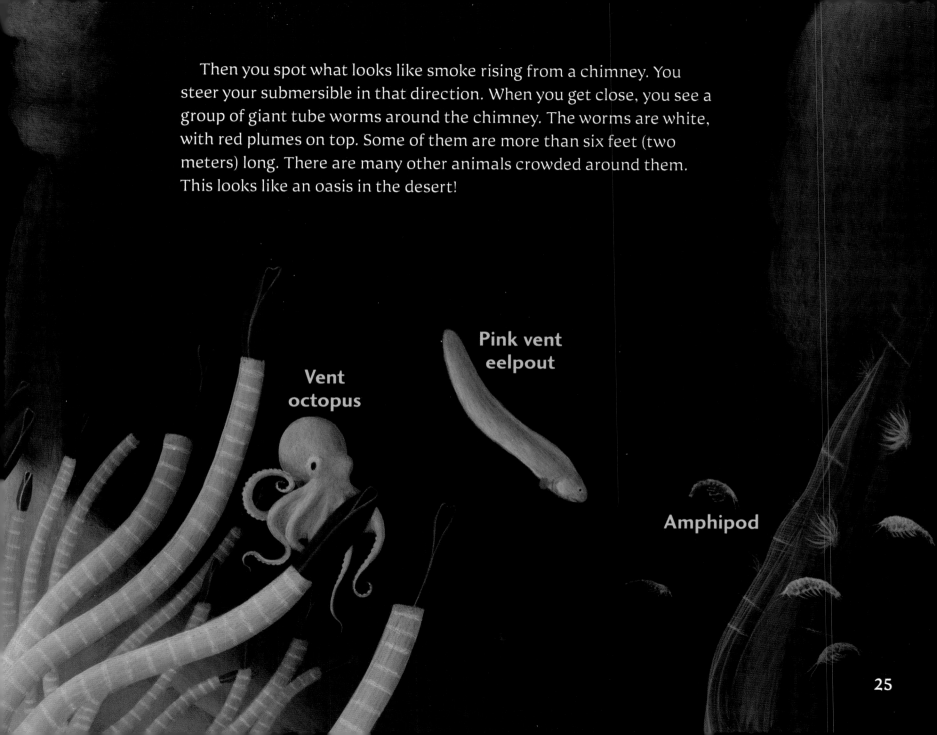

Then you spot what looks like smoke rising from a chimney. You steer your submersible in that direction. When you get close, you see a group of giant tube worms around the chimney. The worms are white, with red plumes on top. Some of them are more than six feet (two meters) long. There are many other animals crowded around them. This looks like an oasis in the desert!

Vent octopus

Pink vent eelpout

Amphipod

The smoking "chimney" is called a **hydrothermal** vent. In certain areas of the ocean floor, cold seawater seeps down through cracks. The water comes into contact with hot rock deep inside the Earth. The water heats up quickly. Minerals from the rock combine with the water. The hot, mineral-rich water shoots up through the cracks, like water volcanoes.

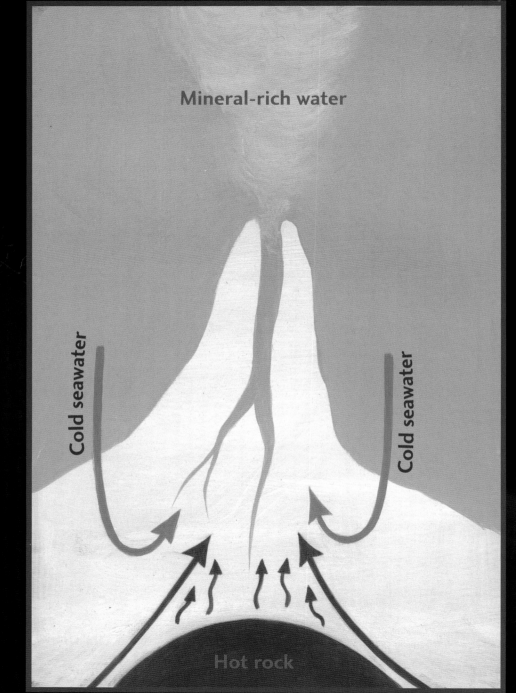

Mineral-rich water

Cold seawater

Cold seawater

Hot rock

The water can be black or white, and it billows up like smoke. The minerals in the water slowly settle out to build tall cones that look like chimneys. When scientists first discovered the animals living around hydrothermal vents, it was like discovering life on another planet!

Scientists long thought that all life depended on light from the sun. Without it, there would be no photosynthesis. Without photosynthesis there could be no food, and no living things could survive. Yet here were animals living in total darkness, without using even a scrap of food from above. How could they possibly do it?

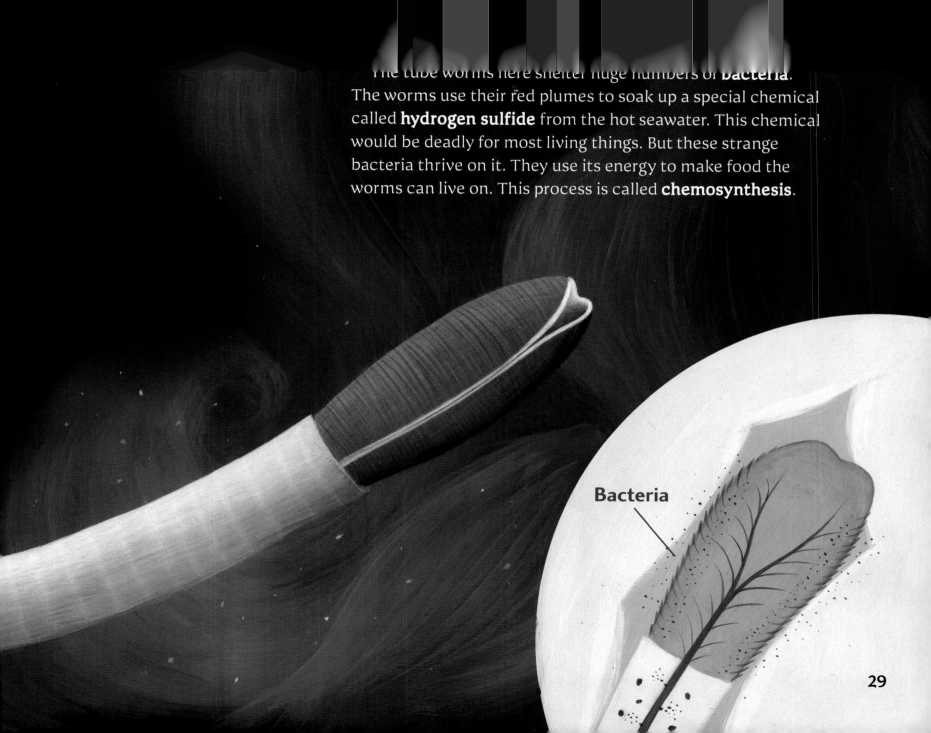

The tube worms here shelter huge numbers of **bacteria**. The worms use their red plumes to soak up a special chemical called **hydrogen sulfide** from the hot seawater. This chemical would be deadly for most living things. But these strange bacteria thrive on it. They use its energy to make food the worms can live on. This process is called **chemosynthesis**.

Bacteria

29

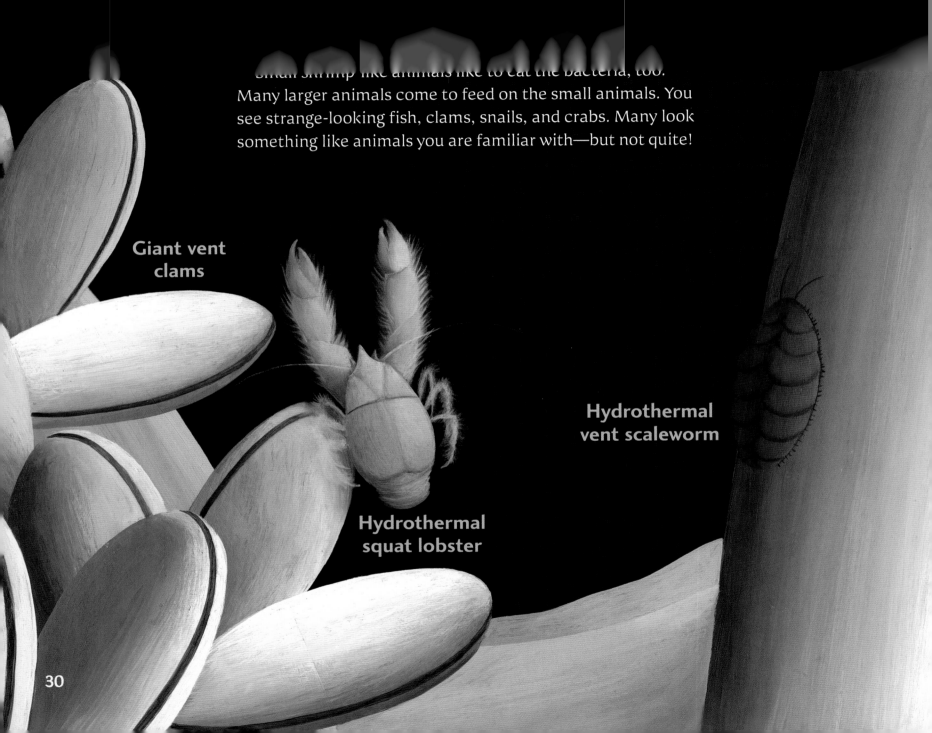

Small shrimp-like animals like to eat the bacteria, too. Many larger animals come to feed on the small animals. You see strange-looking fish, clams, snails, and crabs. Many look something like animals you are familiar with—but not quite!

Giant vent clams

Hydrothermal squat lobster

Hydrothermal vent scaleworm

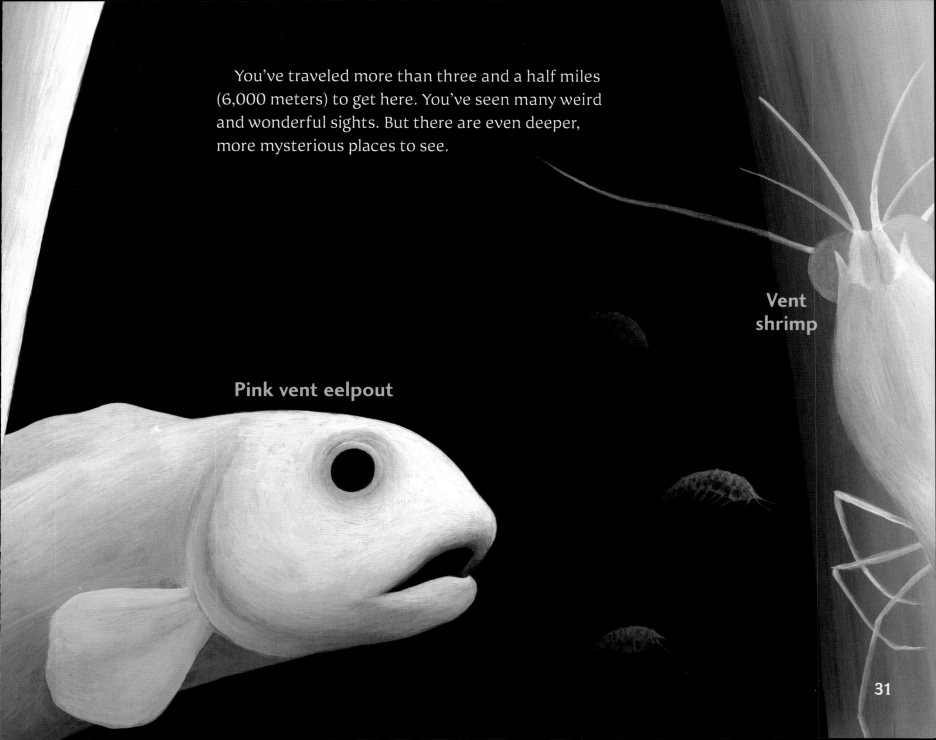

You've traveled more than three and a half miles (6,000 meters) to get here. You've seen many weird and wonderful sights. But there are even deeper, more mysterious places to see.

Vent shrimp

Pink vent eelpout

THE HADAL ZONE

Crisscrossing the ocean are canyons so deep, they would make the Grand Canyon look tiny. The deepest of all is the Mariana Trench, in the western Pacific Ocean. The Grand Canyon is a little over one mile (1,830 meters) deep. The deepest part of the Mariana Trench reaches down nearly seven miles (11,030 meters)!

Sea lilies

Snailfish

Amphipod

Are you ready to dive in? Only a few people have ever taken this journey. As you go, keep a sharp eye out for any signs of life. Scientists using deep-sea cameras have filmed odd kinds of fish, shrimp, sea cucumbers, and more! Even in the deepest, darkest, coldest depths of the ocean, there is life.

Under Pressure!

When you are standing on the beach, you have about 15 pounds of pressure per square inch on your body. You are not underwater, but you are under air! It's called "one atmosphere" of pressure. And you don't feel it at all. It's what you're used to. For every 33 feet (10 meters) you dive down underwater, the pressure increases by one atmosphere.

Imagine trying to stand at the bottom of the Mariana Trench! There the pressure is more than 16,000 pounds per square inch. How do the animals that live there stand it? The pressure inside their bodies is the same as the pressure outside.

You can feel how even a little bit of water exerts some pressure.

To find out, you'll need:

- A long, narrow plastic bag, such as a bread bag
- A large, thick rubber band
- A large bowl of water, or sink, about half full of water

Slip your arm inside the bag. Use the rubber band to seal the top of the bag around your forearm, near your elbow. Then put your arm completely underwater. What happens to the bag? How does it feel?

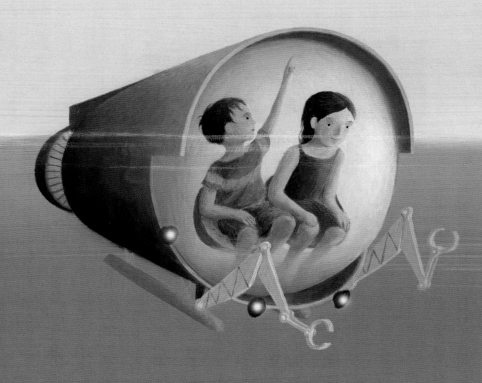

No doubt there are many new life-forms to be discovered here. But it's time to head home. You rise up—from the darkest depths to the sparkling sunlit surface. It has been a long trip, with many amazing sights along the way. Those who go down in submersibles never forget this strange and alien world. But it always feels good to come up into the sunlight again. Back where there's air to breathe, and the pressure is just right for humans!

GLOSSARY

Bacteria (back-TEER-ee-uh): Tiny, single-celled organisms that live everywhere on Earth. There are millions of different kinds of bacteria.

Bioluminescence (BY-oh-LOO-mih-NESS-ents): The production of light by a living thing. Unlike light from the sun or other sources, this is usually a light without heat, or "cold light."

Chemosynthesis (KEE-moh-SIN-thu-sis): The process of making food from carbon dioxide and water, using energy from chemicals rather than the energy of the sun.

Hydrogen sulfide (HI-dro-gin SUL-fide): A colorless gas with the foul odor of rotten eggs. It often occurs with volcanic gasses, and it is easily set on fire and burns quickly.

Hydrothermal (HI-dro-THER-mul): Having to do with water heated by the energy of the Earth. From the Greek words *hydro* (or *hydor*), meaning "water," and *thermos*, meaning "heat."

Photosynthesis (FOE-toe-SIN-thu-sis): The process of making food from carbon dioxide and water, using energy from sunlight.

Phytoplankton (FY-toh-PLANK-ton): A vast multitude of tiny living things float, drift, or swim in the ocean's currents. These are called plankton. Phtyoplankton are plankton that make their own food, through photosynthesis.

Scuba (SKOO-bah): Short for: *S*elf-*c*ontained *u*nderwater *b*reathing *a*pparatus. Scuba gear lets divers breathe air while swimming underwater.

Submersible (sub-MER-si-bul): A small boat or craft especially made to travel underwater. Submersibles are used for deep-sea research.

FIND OUT MORE ABOUT

How to Measure the Deep Dark Sea

The ocean floor was once thought to be just a flat, muddy plain. We now know it's crisscrossed by deep trenches and high mountain ranges. But how did we find out? In 1872, Charles Wyville Thomson, chief scientist aboard the HMS (Her Majesty's Ship) *Challenger*, used a process called "sounding" to measure the ocean's depth at many different locations. You can make your own sounding line to see how it is done.

You'll need:
- A piece of string, about two feet (61 centimeters) long
- A metal washer
- A ruler
- A large bowl of water, or sink filled with water

1. Tie the metal washer to one end of the string. Then, tie a small knot one inch (2.5 centimeters) above the washer. Continue tying knots in the string, spacing them evenly—one inch apart. Use your ruler to make sure your spaces are exact.

2. Toss the washer overboard! And let it sink to the bottom of your bowl of water. Hold the other end of the string up straight. How many inches deep is the water in your bowl? Gently make waves in the water with your hand. What happens to your depth measurement? Does it change?

The *Challenger* scientists used rope and a heavy lead weight instead of string and a washer. They tied their knots every six feet (1.8 meters). That unit of measurement is called a "fathom." They were stunned to find a part of the ocean that was 26,850 feet (8,262 meters), or 4,475 fathoms, deep. (That's a LOT of rope!) They had discovered the Mariana Trench! The deepest part of the Trench is named "Challenger Deep" in their honor.

Today, scientists use sonar to measure the ocean's depths. A sonar device sends a sound wave, or "ping," down through the water. Sound travels through water at a constant rate. The sonar device records the time it takes for the ping to reach the seafloor and bounce, or echo, back. From that information, the scientists can calculate the exact depth of the water in that place.

Hydrothermal vents and cold seeps

www.mbari.org/benthic/coldseeptour.htm

wwf.panda.org/about_our_earth/blue_planet/
deep_sea/vents_seeps/

Submersibles, ROVs, and Landers

www.oceanexplorer.noaa.gov/technology/
subs/subs.html

www.ocean.si.edu/ocean-news/submarines-
robots-exploring-deep-ocean

www.whoi.edu/hades/hadal-lander-b/

This book meets the Common Core State Standards for Science and Technical Subjects. For Common Core resources for this title and others, please visit www.readcommoncore.com.

Be sure to look for all of these books in the **Let's-Read-and-Find-Out** Science series: